ULTIMATE

VICTORY

A DETECTIVE BILL CELLI NOVEL

(SEQUAL TO THE YELLOW CARD)

BY

CARL K. OSBORNE

THIS IS A WORK OF FICTION, ALL NAMES,
PLACES, CHARACTERS, AND INCIDENTS AND
ANY RESEMBLANCE TO ACTUAL EVENTS OR THE
PERSONS LIVING OR DEAD ARE PURELY
COINCIDENTAL.

ACKNOWLEDGEMENTS

TO MY WIFE JANICE WHO HAS READ MY WORK OVER AND OVER AGAIN MAKING APPROPRIATE CORRECTIONS AND CHANGES SO THE BEST PRODUCT REACHES THE READER.

DEDICATION

I DEDICATE THIS BOOK TO ED RUDDY, WHO IS A RETIRED LAPD OFFICER EVEN THOUGHT I AM A CRIMINAL DEFENCE LAWYER, WE BECAME GOOD FRIENDS. HE HAS BEEN ONE OF MY FAVORITE CHARACTERS IN MY PRIOR BOOKS. I WISH HIM WELL.

.

Chapter 1

It was Andrew Tanner's weekend for visitation with his son Carson, who had just turned six years old. Tanner left his office around 5:30 p.m. and took the thirty-minute ride to his ex-wife's house. He and Sandy had divorced two years ago after eight years of marriage.

When he reached the house, he saw Carson standing by the front door with his overnight bag. The boy raced to give Andrew a hug as his dad exited the car. Carson had made it clear he wanted to live with his father, no matter how much his parents had tried to explain to the boy why it wouldn't work. Basically, Andrew traveled a lot for his work, although he hoped one day things might be different and Carson could live with him.

Carson jumped into Andrew's Porsche for the ride down the coast to San Diego. They were headed to Sea World, one of Carson's favorite places. The trip from Santa Monica would take a little over three and a half hours which was not too bad for Friday night rush hour traffic. Happily, the traffic congestion started to break up as they reached San Clemente.

Andrew and Carson were celebrating the let-up of traffic when it happened, a car in the fast lane suddenly swerved, striking the center divider and crossing three lanes just ahead of Andrew's car. Andrew braked to avoid the collision, as the black Chevrolet SUV came to rest on the side of the freeway. Its sole occupant jumped out of the car and ran, jumping a fence which ran alongside the freeway. The SUV driver then ran across a parallel road and disappeared between buildings. Andrew pulled over and parked on the shoulder, as did a couple of other vehicles. His Porsche sat directly behind the disabled SUV. Pulling out his phone, he called 911 to report the crash.

Not frightened by the near crash, Carson thought it was all very exciting and fun—sort of like a movie.

"Stay here in the car," directed Andrew to his son, as he exited his car and walked up to the SUV. Peering through the rear window, he could see what looked like a body lying in the back of the SUV. He immediately opened the rear hatch and with the help of a couple of other people pulled out the body.

Andrew knew immediately that the person was dead. There appeared to be dried blood around a bullet hole in the head. They left the body in the back of the vehicle while they waited for the police to arrive. Andrew estimated the male victim was between the ages of 30 and 35. Interestingly, the victim was wearing a business suit. Andrew again called 911 to report the further discovery of the body in the disabled vehicle.

Andrew did not want his son to see the dead body, so he quickly returned to his car. The two played games until the police arrived. The first to reach the scene was a Highway Patrol officer. Locking

Carson safely inside his car once again,

Andrew approached the patrol car and

explained who he was and that he had

reported the incident. The officer took

down his account of the black SUV and

the man who had exited it.

"That's all I can tell you, Officer

Mack," said Andrew, reading his badge. "I

really need to get back to my six-year-old

son in the car. I definitely do not want him

to see the dead body."

Mack said, "I understand, sir. Please

give me your contact information. You

should expect a call from our office. We will need a written report."

"Of course," responded Andrew, handing his business card to the officer. "I'm a Federal Secret Service officer. I work out of the L.A. area office."

He returned to his car, and the two drove off. It was almost 7 p.m. by that time, but it was still light outside thanks to it being the middle of July. Carson was bugging him to stop that he was hungry, so as soon as they reached San Diego he pulled off the freeway and spotted a McDonald's. Andrew was a health nut and didn't believe in feeding his kid junk food, he decided to make an exception this time.

While at McDonald's, he called his current girlfriend, Barbara, who lived nearby on Coronado Island. They had met about a year ago when President Fred Whitehead had scheduled a campaign speech in San Diego. As a television newscaster for the local ABC affiliate, Barbara had interviewed the President for her news show. Since Andrew was in charge of President Whitehead's protection unit, he needed to obtain the necessary security clearances for the television cast and crew. He and Barbara hit it off right away.

"Hi, it's me. Sorry we are running late," said Andrew who went on to explain what had happened on the trip down. "We should be at your condo within an hour."

Barbara's condo was a block from the Del Coronado Hotel and faced the beach. Carson loved to visit and take rides on Barbara's boat around the Navy ships that sat in the harbor.

Although the weekend had gotten a bumpy start, the rest was a total success.

Carson loved Sea World and was happy to be out with his dad, whom he called the 'president's bodyguard' when bragging to his schoolmates. Sunday came too soon. Andrew had promised his ex-wife that he would have Carson back by five.

As they were driving back, Andrew said, "It might not be cool to say anything to your mom about the car accident on the freeway. It would only make her nervous."

"I understand, Dad. It's our secret."

"I love you and I want you to protect Mom."

"I know. Just like you protect the President."

Andrew smiled and said, "Yeah, something like that."

Chapter 2

Highway Patrol Officer Franks was the first to respond to the 911 call. He had the vehicle towed to an impound lot after the body had been removed, unaware the FBI would be taking over the case after the victim had been identified. He ran the vehicle plates, and the DMV verified that the registered owner was William Wallace who he called notifying him that his car had been involved in an accident and was being held at the impound lot. And that since a dead body had been found in the vehicle, it was being held by law enforcement pending investigation.

When FBI Agent Roger Smith was advised that Wallace had been contacted, he was livid. This could have compromised his investigation. He needed to act quickly, contacting his surveillance team to make contact with Wallace at his residence.

Wallace was surprised to find the FBI at his door, but he invited them in. They informed him that FBI Agent Roger Smith wanted to have a conversation with him.

"What is this all about?" asked Wallace. "Is it about the auto accident? I don't understand."

"Agent Smith will explain," responded one of the agents. "Right now, we need to take you to FBI headquarters, sir."

"Do you know who I am?" said Wallace, resisting the agent's request.

Agent Ford replied, "Whoever you are doesn't matter, Mr. Wallace. Please cooperate."

"It's Sunday. I was planning to take my family to the club for Sunday brunch. Can't we handle this over the phone?"

"Sorry to ruin your plans, but this is important. I must insist you come with us," said Ford.

"Okay, but I don't like this one bit. This better be as important as you say. I'll drive myself and follow you."

About an hour later, an extremely annoyed Wallace was seated in front of Roger Smith.

"I appreciate you giving up your Sunday, Mr. Wallace," said the FBI agent.

"This better be good," said Wallace. "Your agents didn't exactly give me a choice."

"I'll try and be brief," replied Smith. "You're the owner of a black Chevrolet SUV?"

"Yes."

"Well, it was involved in an accident, and whoever was driving fled the scene. A body was found in the vehicle. Do you know who was driving your SUV?"

"I can't tell you who was driving the car. It's a company vehicle that we keep parked at our office building. A lot of employees have access to it, we have over 40 employees working for the company. Tell me, why is the FBI interested? Does it have something to do with the victim?"

"I can't say, but I need you to keep this information to yourself. I'm going to send some agents to your office on Monday to review your employee records. Please advise them to cooperate."

"I don't have a problem with that, but they should interview the garage attendants. They might know who drove the car out."

"That's very helpful, Mr. Wallace. I hope I didn't ruin your Sunday."

Wallace said he understood and thanked the FBI agent for being brief. Before the meeting, Smith had done his due diligence on Wallace which included a personal background of him and his family. He had grown up in L.A., graduated from Princeton and was married with two grown children. William Wallace was well past retirement age, but still acted as chairman of the board of his investment company. There was nothing in his background of a criminal nature.

Chapter 3

When Andrew arrived at his office on Monday morning, the receptionist advised him that he had a phone message on his desk from FBI Agent Roger Smith.

After making himself a cup of coffee, Andrew returned the call, thinking it had to be related to the accident over the weekend.

"Mr. Tanner, thanks for returning my call. I understand you were a witness to a car crash on the 405 last Friday," said Smith.

"Yes," said Andrew. "I was expecting a call."

"I'm the lead investigator concerning the dead body discovered in the vehicle," said Smith.

"That was horrible," said Andrew. "Do you know who it was?"

"I can't discuss it over the phone. I can fill you in when we meet in person. Can you come to my office on the seventh floor in the Federal Building?"

"I'm on the third floor," answered Andrew. I'll come up as soon as I finish my coffee."

When Andrew arrived minutes later, he was directed to Smith's office. When he was greeted by the FBI agent, Andrew guessed that Smith was a very in-shape 50 year old his gray hair the only hint to his age.

With both of them in federal law enforcement, Smith felt comfortable disclosing everything that he knew so far about the case, including the fact that the dead body belonged to a DEA agent who had gone undercover two years ago to infiltrate a drug cartel in Mexico. The undercover agent had been placed into the jail system in a federal institution where some other cartel operatives were being housed, and, during the year that followed, he had made friends with them. When he was released from prison, the undercover agent had been invited to Mexico to meet one of the leaders of the cartel. Since he was an American who spoke perfect Spanish, the cartel thought he would be an asset in their smuggling operation into the United States.

"Somehow, he was found out," said Smith. "We don't know how his cover was blown, but that's why he ended up dead. We have little to go on at the moment, but we do know who owns the crashed vehicle. We assumed that he was the driver who ran, but upon meeting with him, we discovered it was a company car available to several employees, and it doesn't appear that the owner had any knowledge of the crash. So far, we have kept this quiet and out of the press."

"What can I do to help?" asked Andrew.

"It would help greatly if you could identify the driver. Did you get a good look?"

"It happened quickly, but I did see him. I would say he was in his early 30s,

Caucasian, he had short black hair and was approximately six feet tall. I remember he had an athletic build and was well dressed—in a business suit, which struck me as odd for someone fleeing."

"That definitely does not fit the description of William Wallace, the car's owner. He is 62 years old and the boss of a real estate investment firm which owned many high-rise buildings in the downtown L.A. area. From everything we know, he also seems to be very politically connected."

Chapter 4

After the meeting with Tanner and Smith, other agents arrived at Wallace's investment firm to help in the search for the SUV's driver. Their arrival was not a surprise since, Wallace had previously warned his staff that they were coming and asked for everyone's cooperation.

Now that Smith had a description of the driver, he was able to share that information with Wallace's operations officer who then researched the files for any possible matches. He pulled out ten employee profiles that came closest to fitting the description of the driver of the vehicle. Each file had a picture and a resume, along with the annual reports of their productivity on the job. Smith was impressed. It took a couple of hours to review the material.

Next, the agents went to the garage to interview the attendants about the possible driver of the car. Two of them were familiar with the vehicle and agreed that the last time they had seen it was about a week ago, but they couldn't recall who was actually driving it out of the garage.

Smith showed each of the garage attendant's photos of the ten employees they had extracted from the files, hoping to refresh their memories. Max, one of the attendants, thought it might have been Felipe Serena.

Agent Cannon returned to the office, hoping to interview Serena. Interestingly, Felipe Serena had failed to show up for work that morning. He asked the receptionist to call him. The cell phone went directly to voicemail. Cannon contacted his boss that Serena was absent from work. Smith there upon contacted Washington to do some research on Felipe Serena.

An email arrived with the background results. Felipe Serena was a green card holder. He was 32 years old and was from Mexico. Serena had been recruited by the Wallace Company. Evidently, his family was filthy rich and had invested millions of dollars with Wallace. It all seemed to be above board.

Even if Serena had been the driver, it still didn't explain what he doing with a dead undercover DEA agent, thought Smith. His last known address was in Century City so Smith decided to ask LAPD to check out his residence. He placed a call to Chief of Police Phil La Greca and explained the situation.

Since the event was a homicide investigation, Bill Celli, head detective of the Homicide Division, was given the task. Celli opted to send a couple of his detectives to Felipe Serena's condo on the pretext that someone had reported that they heard a gunshot coming from the floor his condo was on. Detectives Sandra Salute and Jerry Forman were briefed on the situation, along with the fact that the FBI was also involved. They were given a photo of Felipe Serena.

When they arrived at the address on the Avenue of the Stars, they located the condo on the 16th floor.

"This place is big money," said Detective Sandra Salute. "I bet the cheapest condo in here is worth a few million or more. Who is this guy? I guess that's why we are here—to figure it out."

The detectives knocked on the doors of all four units on the floor, including Serena's. Two of the condos answered the door, and Forman gave them the spiel about a report of a gunshot. No one had heard anything.

Salute asked one of the occupants if they knew who lived in unit D.

"That's Felipe's condo," said the neighbor. "He's nice enough, but we hardly ever see him."

Salute returned to the ground floor and located the office manager of the building, where she explained the need to check inside unit D.

"It's an emergency," stated Salute. "Someone could be dead or injured."

The building manager, Ed Saul, gave her a dubious look. He found it strange that anything she was suggesting was a possibility.

"If you don't cooperate, Mr. Saul, I'll be forced to call my boss. I suggest you do the right thing."

"No need to do that," replied Saul. "I'll be right up with the key to let you in."

"Thank you. That is a wise move," said the detective.

Once the door was open, Salute and Forman were stunned by the panoramic view of the Pacific Ocean in the distance. The 2,000-square-foot interior was spotless. Asking Saul to stay positioned by the front door, the two detectives slowly made their way through each room. They noted that the refrigerator only contained a couple of six packs of beer. Some men's clothes were hung in one of the bedroom closets, though a search of various drawers found nothing of interest. A pad of paper by the phone had a name, Felix Santos, along with a local phone number. They wrote down the information before leaving.

As they walked past the building manager, the detectives held up their hands to show him they had removed nothing from the condo. When they got back to the squad car, Salute called Celli.

"Bill, we found nothing in the condo. In fact, it doesn't look occupied. There was a notepad with a phone number and a name Felix Santos on it?"

Celli was stunned by the mention of Felix Santos. Without answering, he thanked the detectives and hung up. He needed to digest this possible connection with a former case. He asked Casey, his new secretary, to pull the files on Gray and Valentine. "You'll find them in the unsolved case storage, Casey."

A half hour later, Casey placed the files in front of the detective. He looked up and said, "Please close my door on your way out. I don't want to be disturbed."

Celli read each file from cover to cover, remembering each detail of the frustrating cases. The name of Felix Santos and Roberto Torres came up numerous times, as he remembered it like it had all gone down yesterday. He got on the phone to Steinberg, the computer whiz of the department, and asked him to determine the owner of the phone number found in Serena's condo.

Steinberg, also a genius with social media, got back ten minutes later with the phone's owner: Roberto Torres.

This was better than he could have imagined. Smiling to himself, Celli called FBI Agent Roger Smith and asked permission to follow-up on this new lead.

"Go ahead, but please keep me informed," replied Smith.

When Salute and Forman returned to headquarters, they found the unsolved files on Celli's desk and a Celli smiling contentedly.

"Why the smile, boss?" asked Jerry Forman.

"Guess who the phone number belongs to?" answered Celli. Forman had no idea.

"That's okay. You won't believe this. It is none other than Roberto Torres. Does that sound familiar?"

"That explains the files on your desk," said Forman who definitely remembered the infamous cartel boss.

"I have his address, but there's nothing that Steinberg has found out other than he has entered the U.S. from Mexico."

"Wow, but how should we proceed?" asked Forman. "It's the Fed's case."

"The Feds don't know about our unsolved murders right now. I got their permission to continue our investigation. I want to put on a 24-hour surveillance team to watch the targeted residence and to also video record any movements. We will also need a backup team to follow anyone leaving the premises. Forman, you pick the teams. I want daily reports."

After the detective left to organize the surveillance, Celli reviewed the old cases one more time. Was this his chance to close one case while solving another? Wouldn't that be sweet.

Chapter 5

The property targeted for surveillance was located in a gated community off of Mulholland Drive in Encino. Mountain Gate Estates consisted of twenty-five large residence homes that could easily be described as mansions. The gated aspect complicated any type of surveillance without setting off red flags.

The property in question was leased by Wallace's real estate investment company, which meant nothing to Celli at the time. However, they knew that notifying security would most likely mean security would alert the occupants of the residence.

Celli brought Chief La Greca up to date on the case and requested the use of the department's drones for surveillance.

La Greca said, "You can use them, but remember they must be at least 500 feet off the ground. Otherwise, you are going to need a warrant."

"No problem, Chief. Let's give it a try."

The new plan was to have the drone fly above the authorized 500 feet and video the property, sending the pictures to a control center. The control center would then notify Celli of any movement to or from the property. Anyone leaving would be followed by Forman's team waiting outside of the community gate.

Chapter 6

After the unexpected car crash, Felipe Serena had panicked. Jumping over the freeway fencing, he had run through a nearby neighborhood, finally reaching the Pacific Coast Highway and a Starbucks. He knew he needed to calm down and think.

He ordered a coffee and took a seat in a tucked away corner to think. He would call Joey Medina at the residence, explain what happened and ask him what to do next. Joey would know.

"Where are you?" asked Medina, listening to Serena's rambling.

"I have no idea...a Starbucks."

"Well, ask someone. I'll wait."

"Okay, Joey," said Serena after asking the barista. "I'm in San Onofre, you know near that nuclear plant north of San Diego."

"Listen to me," said Medina. "Go find a motel, then call me back. I'll have Federico pick you up. Do not panic, understand?"

Find out what happened to the body. We can't have anything lead back to us."

On Monday morning, William Wallace arrived at the office early to place a call on the landline to Felix Santos.

"Felix, the FBI is asking questions about who was driving one of our company cars involved in an auto accident last Friday," said Wallace. "The driver ran away, and a dead body was found in the car. What the hell is going on?"

"Do they know who the driver was?" replied Santos.

"I don't know, but when they are going to show up at my office later this morning, they asked us to provide a list of names of employees who had access to the car…You have to keep me out of all this."

"It's not your problem, but you could have had the vehicle reported stolen," said Santos.

"Sorry I didn't, but I was taken by surprise. It's too late now. I don't believe they have any kind of description of the driver, but I'm sure they will be contacting everyone on that list."

"Okay, I'll take care of it from here," said Santos.

Santos called Roberto Torres next. "I think we are in the clear, but we need to get Serena back to L.A. fast. The FBI has a list and he is probably on it. The FBI will be knocking on his door at any time. He'll need an alibi for his whereabouts from Friday to today."

Art Ramos was sent to the safehouse in San Diego to pick up Felipe Serena and return him to the Mountain Gate property on Mulholland, as instructed by Torres. By the time they arrived, Celli's drones were hovering above the mansion and a surveillance team waited nearby the entrance to the enclave of estates.

The drone forwarded video of the vehicle driven by Ramos entering the estate. Two males were visible inside, one in the driver seat and the other in the front passenger seat.

Celli was there waiting when the still photographs taken from the drone's video arrived. He compared the pictures against the photo of Felipe Serena. It was a match. He called in Forman who concurred with his observation.

"That's him," said Forman, "but what's our next step? It's not our case."

"We don't know where the crime took place, only that the body was discovered in Orange or San Diego County," replied Celli.

"We need to turn over all of our investigation reports to Smith," said Forman. "Maybe we can work with him since our own murder suspects have surfaced."

"Jerry, I think we should keep that to ourselves. Let the FBI go ahead and do what they can with their own resources."

"Okay, Bill, whatever you say. You are the boss."

Chapter 7

Celli met with Smith at FBI headquarters, anxious to share his investigative reports. Smith was all smiles after reading the results.

"Thank you, Detective Celli, for your help in locating Serena," said the FBI agent.

"Happy we could help," replied Celli. "My people still have the property under surveillance."

"Great! Give me 24 hours and then you can pull your team off."

"I would appreciate it if you could keep me in the loop," said Celli.

"Of course, Detective. I hope I can call on you for assistance if needed in the future."

"No problem," said Celli, shaking the agent's hand.

Chapter 8

Felipe Serena was escorted into the study of the estate where Roberto Torres and Miguel Ayala were awaiting his arrival.

Seeing the two powerful men only made him more nervous. He had fucked up and he knew it was serious this time. Probably the only thing that had kept him alive up until now was his family connections in Mexico, but that could only buy him so many screw ups.

The grilling began immediately. No niceties were exchanged. The grueling questions continued for a couple of hours with Torres and Ayala taking turns. They were trying to learn everything about what had happened in detail. It was the only way to assess the threat to the company, and the man in the hot seat was the only one who could answer these questions.

Torres and Ayala were fully aware that the FBI had identified Serena as the driver. They needed him to disappear, and they had to get him out of the house. Not knowing if they were under surveillance, it was agreed that they would wait until after dark. The plan was simple. They ordered some food to be delivered from a local restaurant in Van Nuys. Frank Piazza, the owner of the restaurant, was connected. Torres explained the situation to him, and the plan was set.

At about 8 p.m. the restaurant delivery van pulled up to the security guardhouse. A few minutes later, it entered the property. This part had been observed by the surveillance team, however, when the van disappeared into the community, they could not be sure of its destination since the drone had been taken down.

When the van arrived, it was directed to the rear of the house. When it exited the complex minutes later, Serena was safely hidden in the rear of the delivery truck completely out of sight. One of the surveillance teams followed the van back to the restaurant, reporting in when they arrived as instructed. Their orders were to stay there and send one from the team into the restaurant for some takeout and observe the activity. Twenty minutes later, the undercover detective left, takeout food in hand. Nothing unusual had been observed and there was no sign of Serena.

Serena had remained in the delivery van until close of business. After securing the surroundings, he was placed in the trunk of Frank Piazza's personal car. He remained there until reaching the restaurant owner's residence in Pasadena. Once there, Serena was picked up by one of the company soldiers and driven to the Van Nuys Airport to board a waiting private plane that would fly him out of the country.

The following day, Celli's team was pulled off surveillance, surrendering the investigation to the FBI.

Chapter 9

After his meeting with Celli, Smith was of the opinion that Wallace was more involved than he had let on. He couldn't ignore the fact that the estate Serena was brought to was owned by Wallace's company. He needed to figure out exactly how he was connected to the unsavory characters who seemed to be occupying the premises.

By this time, he had been in contact with Victor Cortez, the head of the DEA in Los Angeles. Smith requested all of the DEA reports concerning Phil Dawson's undercover activities.

When Cortez hesitated to share the reports, Smith raised his voice and said, "Listen, your man is dead and I need to know why! I need to know everything leading up to his death. I can go over your head, but I don't think you want me to do that. Just what are you hiding?"

"Okay, calm down. I'll call Washington and get the okay," said Cortez.

"In the meantime, tell me this," continued Smith. "Do you know a William Wallace?"

"Yes, I know who he is," replied Cortez. "We think he and his company are money-laundering for a group of Mexican cartels, investing drug money into larger-than-life real estate projects. Once I get the okay from Washington, I can fill you in."

"Sorry for losing my temper," said the FBI agent, "but I don't like it one bit when one of our good guys is killed doing his job."

Chapter 10

Francisco Rodriguez, who had just

been promoted to the head of the Justice

Department, got involved after receiving

an interesting telephone call from FBI

agent Roger Smith. Smith informed him

that the FBI was investigating the murder

of a DEA undercover officer and that he

was getting stonewalled by the head of

the DEA's office in L.A.

Not even a day went by before the

FBI agent received a call from Victor

Cortez.

"I think I have everything you need in our files on Dawson's undercover work," said Cortez. "Can you send someone around to pick up the files?"

Smith was happy to oblige, and three hours later the files were on his desk. The reports revealed that Dawson was the grandson of the U.S. ambassador to Mexico, and he had spent his summers as a youth with his grandfather in Mexico City where he became fluent in the Spanish language. When he was sixteen years old, his grandfather was recalled from the post, so his visits had stopped. His parents lived in Richmond, Virginia and were both retired military and have stayed actively connected with Pentagon brass.

After his high school graduation, Dawson had been accepted to West Point, where he met Wilson Scott. The two classmates became fast friends. Scott dropped out of West Point in his senior year when he was recruited by the Drug Enforcement Agency. Scott convinced Dawson to do the same despite his parents' objections. Both went through a year of training after which they became field officers and partners. Over the next five years, they had traveled the globe seeking out sources of illegal drug trafficking into the U.S., making numerous arrests and becoming the pride of the agency.

One day, Dawson received a telephone call from Washington D.C. The Director of the DEA wanted him to come to Washington and meet. Dawson's meeting with Director Brooks would be lifechanging. Brooks explained that the agency was setting up an undercover task force to infiltrate cartel activity.

"Since joining the DEA, you have made quite a name for yourself," said

Brooks. "And your being fluent in Spanish makes you a prime candidate for the job."

Brooks went on to explain the details of his undercover duties. The plan was to place him deep into the cartel, assuming an undercover name and history. He would be placed in a federal prison in Arizona which routinely housed convicted cartel drug smugglers. In there, he was to make friends and build relationships and confidence. The plan involved no one, except the cell block supervisor who was his inside contact, knowing about his true identity.

Dawson had accepted the undercover assignment. It took nearly a year before he felt comfortable enough to advise his contact that cartel inmates had asked him to join the organization. He told his cellmates that he would be up for parole soon and would definitely like an introduction to the cartel.

A few days before his release date, Dawson was given a contact number to call in Mexico. He was told to say that Pedro asked him to call. With the undercover name of Jack and the DEA-created dossier that made up his family life as well as his criminal history, any investigation by the cartel would make him look legitimate.

After his release, "Jack" made contact and was invited to Mexico City. It took about a week there before the top cartel brass, as well as Felix Santos, the head of the Mexican Mafia, accepted the undercover agent into the organization.

His new life began. Dawson reported on his activities to his handler every thirty days, usually meeting in a public place such as a sporting event. For safety reasons, all of his reports were verbal, but his handler would usually record their conversations then turn over the recordings to the DEA. Things were going well and he was moving up in the organization. However, one day he failed to show up for his meeting with his handler, and for the following four months there had been no contact—until his body showed up in the back of a SUV on the 405 freeway.

After reading the reports, Smith called Cortez. "I've read the reports that you provided, Mr. Cortez. I take it they were prepared by his handler since there were no names mentioned in the reports. Did he provide the names of the people he was working for?"

The answer was 'yes'.

"Can you give me the names from the top down?" responded Smith.

"I was told to cooperate with you," said Cortez, "so I guess I can. Felix Santos, the head of the Mexican Mafia, had the last word on the drug cartels' activities, and David Molina and Ray Flores were the heads of the two major drug cartels operating out of Mexico City and Acapulco. Dawson worked under the supervision of the Ochoa brothers, Miguel and Joe, who were based in Tijuana and San Diego. They were responsible for getting the drugs across the border into

California and distributed to various dealers throughout the Western states, California, Oregon, Washington and Nevada. There were five to six sub-cartel groups that performed the same function in different parts of the country, each group operating independently from the others. That way if one group went down, the others were protected. Dawson could only provide us information on the Ochoa brothers' contacts."

"Any other names?" asked Smith.

"Yes… Joey Medina, Alfred Lopez and Miquel Ayala. At the time of his disappearance, he was working on getting information about the other groups in the organization."

"I need to speak with his handler," said Smith.

"I'll have to clear that with D.C. since he is now assigned to another operative."

"Let me ask you this. Have you ever heard the names Felipe Serena or Roberto Torres?"

"No, I don't know those names," said Cortez.

"Okay, please let me know when I can speak with Dawson's handler."

Later that day, Smith met with U.S. attorney Warren Baron about getting a search warrant for the Mountain Gate property.

After listening to the FBI agent, Baron said, "I think Federal Judge Rubin is your man. I will need a declaration from you and Detective Bill Celli. Once you get those to me, I'll walk them over to Rubin's courtroom."

Just three days later, Smith had a search warrant for the premises, as well as an arrest warrant for Felipe

Serena.

Smith, accompanied by seven U.S.

Marshals and crime lab personnel,

swooped down on the residence. As they

passed through security at the entrance

to Mountain Gate, one of the guards

called Wallace's office and advised him

that U.S. Marshals were headed towards

his property with a search warrant.

Wallace, not really aware of what was

going on at the estate, was shaken. He

had put his full trust in Santos. He

immediately called Santos in a panic.

"No worries," responded Santos. "The residence is spotless."

"Well then, why are U.S. Marshals there?"

"You're covered," said Santos. "Let me worry about it."

Chapter 11

As Smith and his search team reached the target premises, he checked the time. It was 10 a.m. and they had to finish their search before 5 p.m. according to the court's parameters. He hoped that would be enough time.

As they approached the door of the estate, one of the Marshals began videotaping the proceedings. Smith knocked on the front door, and yelled, "FBI! We have a search warrant. Open the door!"

After waiting three minutes without a response, Smith gave the okay to two of the U.S. Marshals armed with battering rams to smash in the door. Upon entering the premises, the team began the search for occupants. None were found. Although he had an arrest warrant for Felipe Serena, Smith knew that was unlikely to happen today. He assigned members of the search team to check each room thoroughly, looking for any evidence, at the same time cautioning them not to touch anything until the lab techs examined their findings.

After three hours of searching inside the estate, no useful evidence had been discovered. Not overlooking any possibility, Smith sent three Marshals to search the garage and the surrounding area. While checking inside a tool box, one of the Marshals found a gun which he photographed along with the tool box. The lab techs dusted the tool box and the weapon and also fingerprinted a box of ammo nearby. The gun and ammo were then bagged and placed in an evidence envelope.

Feeling encouraged, the search of the garage continued. Looking up, a Marshal spotted a rope hanging from a beam. Looking closer at the rope, he discovered what could be bloodstains. They carefully removed the rope and placed it in an evidence envelope.

The lab techs continued dusting each room in the house for fingerprints, discovering a multitude of prints to be analyzed. The tedious process was finally over right before the team's 5 p.m. deadline. There was just enough time to string yellow tape across the damaged front door, announcing that the property was now considered a crime scene. Smith placed two Marshals on site to prevent anyone from entering or tampering with the crime scene.

The initial lab results came in quickly and revealed that the weapon found was in fact the weapon that had shot and killed Dawson. In addition, the blood found on the rope matched Dawson's blood type. Fingerprints were still being run through the FBI database.

Upon receiving the first lab results, Smith contacted Cortez, sharing what they had found so far. Francisco Rodriguez was also notified of the findings that seemed clear to Smith: the DEA agent had most likely been killed in the garage area of the residence. When the FBI agent asked Rodriguez how the case should proceed, his boss directed him to consult with the head of the DEA and his immediate boss.

Smith was anxious to get the fingerprint report. It could be a game changer.

Chapter 12

Over the next few days, Rodriguez met with both the head of the FBI and the head of the DEA to get their respective plans on how they would handle the investigation. The meeting was contentious with the DEA chief acting extremely hostile. He felt that the DEA should be in charge since that one of their agents was the victim. He was also concerned that other officers in the DEA could be exposed if the FBI was involved.

The last thing Rodriguez wanted was to get into a pissing match. He decided to contact Celli and explain his conflicted position. After airing his concerns, Rodriguez came up with his own plan.

"Bill, would you be willing to head up a task force to investigate the murder of the DEA agent?"

"Of course, I would, Francisco, but you know I would have to clear this with the Chief. However, it seems clear to me that the facts show that DEA agent Dawson was killed in our jurisdiction. I will take this on with one stipulation—that I only report to you and that whatever the FBI and the DEA have must be turned over to my office."

Francisco smiled to himself. "It's a deal. You talk to the Chief, and I'll plan to be in L.A. next week. I'll set up a joint meeting with everyone to get the ball rolling."

When Celli outlined Francisco's proposal to Chief La Greca, he was totally onboard, just as the detective had predicted.

Chapter 13

Now it was time for Celli to call in his entire Homicide team to let them know about what was sure to be an immense investigation. What came next would involve a lot of team hours and commitment, but it was an exciting challenge.

Celli was excited to be in the position of not only solving the Dawson murder, but also of quite possibly solving a cold case which involved some of the same suspects. He had asked his personal assistant Casie to make copies of all the investigative reports, including the cold case files involving the murders of David Gray and Coach Valentine. At the meeting, the reports were handed out to the detectives in the Homicide Division. Each detective was instructed to read the reports and write a brief summary with their thoughts. He gave them one week to complete their briefings, in preparation for the meeting with Rodriguez.

During this time, the FBI still controlled the crime scene. Agent Smith suggested that Celli's team step in, but Celli declined.

"I know you are anxious to let your people go, but let's wait until my meeting with Rodriguez next week. After that, my team can take over."

 Regardless of his words to Smith, Celli wasn't wasting any time preparing to take over the crime scene. He sent detectives Salute and Forman to the Foothill Security Company, the outfit who provide the security at Mountain Gate Estates. He instructed them to interview the security personnel and obtain videotape footage from the surveillance cameras.

Foothill compiled a list of thirty security personnel who had worked at Mountain Gate during the last six months. The company also turned over six months of video surveillance tapes and the records of all the people entering and leaving the property for the same period. However, there was a complication the detectives had not anticipated—a rear exit just for property owners was not monitored by security or surveillance cameras.

The six boxes of records provided by Mountain Gate's security was stacked in Celli's office. The head detective assigned detectives Harden and Stanley the job of searching through each box and creating a list of names of all the visitors and occupants who had gone through the guard station entrance with a destination of the residence in question. After the process of separating them from all the others, the box count was down to two.

Detectives Salute, Forman and Elliott were assigned the responsibility of interviewing the security personnel to find out what they knew about the individuals going to and from the residence in question.

Out of the thirty interviewed, ten refused to answer their questions. Those refusing shared the same feeling that nothing good was taking place at the residence and a fear that if it got out that they were helping the cops, their lives and that of their families could be in danger.

The remaining twenty interviewed were cooperative and claimed that they didn't have any suspicions about the property. They all agreed that the property was generally occupied by three to five males, mostly of Hispanic origin. The security personnel had been told that the men were out-of-town employees of the company and that there had never been a problem up until now. They were not told that a murder had taken place or that the FBI was investigating the occupants, but rather to expect a lot of activity in the near future.

Photos from the security company's files were forwarded to the FBI database. They totaled sixty in all; at least half were identified as Mexican nationals. It turned out seven were under investigation by the DEA as members of the Mexican Mafia. About twenty-one were not in the database.

Celli made his list for the meetings coming up with Rodriguez, hoping that the DEA and FBI would be able to provide more information on those individuals. Celli also wanted to interview William Wallace, but he knew this had to be approached carefully because of the man's status in the community. He decided to first ask Chief La Greca for permission.

"I would not make any moves on Wallace until after your meeting with Rodriguez," advised the Chief.

"Chief, you do know that Roberto Torres and Felix Santos are big players in this. If you remember, those names were prevalent in the Gray and Valentine homicides. I can't wait to get my feet wet."

"You'll have your chance soon, Bill."

"I just hope you're right, Chief."

Chapter14

The joint meeting organized by Francisco Rodriguez took place over a two-day period. The discussions began with each agency making a case for their right to lead the task force. Listening to their arguments, Celli soon realized this was just another government bureaucracy power grab that was going nowhere.

Finally, Rodriguez put an end to the ridiculous and unproductive posturing. "Gentlemen, this is the way it is going to go. Celli's unit will be taking the lead. If I hear that either the FBI or the DEA is not cooperating, someone will be looking for another job." The room became silent.

The first order of business was showing DEA Chief Chris Patton the still photographs that had been identified by the FBI database, as well as the fourteen not found. Patton was able to identify eight. One of the eight was Wilson Scott, an active agent for the DEA.

"How did you acquire these photos?" asked Patton, visibly shaken.

 "These are all individuals who went through security prior to going to the property in question as their destination," said Celli. "Were you surprised to see Scott's photo?"

"Yes," stated Patton.

"I request that you do not contact him," cautioned Celli. "However, I would like a background check on him. If there is any chance he has any involvement in this case, it is important that he is not alerted to the fact we are investigating his ties."

"That won't be a problem, detective. I've already given Detective Forman all of our investigative files involving Dawson's undercover work."

Francisco added, "That's the spirit."

"My office will also be available to you, Detective Celli, for any assistance you might need," stated FBI agent Smith.

 By the end of the second day of meetings, everything seemed to be resolved. In celebration, the group happily accepted an evening invitation for dinner and drinks at the LA Country Club as guests of Chief La Greca.

Chapter15

Felix Santos had invited William Wallace to meet at his hacienda just outside of Mexico City. He knew it was important to make sure Wallace was in a calm and stable state of mind. His current anxiety would surely be picked up by detectives. The two had been business partners for many years and it was a perfect arrangement. Wallace had provided the cartel with a foolproof way of cleaning their drug money, and Santos wanted to keep it that way.

Before Wallace's arrival, Santos demanded a meeting with everyone involved in the Dawson murder. The main agenda—finding out how Dawson had been discovered as an undercover narc and why he was not discovered sooner. He wanted the complete story. Everyone was there. Roberto Torres started off the meeting with his detailed explanation of the day.

"I was there the day Dawson showed up for a meeting at the Mountain Gate property to discuss new avenues for getting our product across the border," said Torres. "Wilson Scott, who is on our payroll operating out of the Miami DEA office, he reports to us on gaps in shipping lanes in the Caribbean so as to avoid the Coast Guard and Navy patrols looking for drug smugglers. He had been invited to the meeting as well. He arrived and was being introduced to everyone. But it got really weird when he was introduced to Dawson. We all picked up on the look on Dawson's face when Wilson walked in. You could tell he was shaken, even though they both acted as if this was the very first time they'd ever met."

Torres took a drink of water and continued. "After a couple of minutes, Wilson excused himself from the room, and, as he walked out, he asked me if he could talk to me privately. Once we were out of earshot, he explained that he knew Dawson and that he was DEA. Wilson admitted that he had not seen or spoken to him for a few years. Frankly, I was blind sided. Dawson had come highly recommended by other members of the cartel who met him while he was serving jail time in federal prison. They had no idea. I asked Scott to find out what Dawson was doing here and who he reported to."

Torres continued. "Scott was worried, with good reason, that Dawson could blow his relationship with us and report him to the DEA. He wanted us to take him down immediately. When we came back to the meeting, Scott told the others about Dawson's true identity, although Dawson flatly denied it. But the others weren't buying his story. Joey Medina and Miguel Ayala grabbed him and wrestled him to the ground. They took him into the garage where they tied him up with some rope. They worked him over, but they couldn't get him to admit anything. After a couple of hours of not getting anywhere, I put an end to it. I produced a gun and told Wilson to prove his allegiance to us—that one shot in the head would do it. Scott took the gun from me, put it to Dawson's head and fired one round, killing him instantly."

"After the killing, Scott promised he would find out who his handler was and get as much information as he could without alerting anyone."

Wilson Scott, also present at the Mexico meeting, was painfully reliving the day he had killed his fellow DEA agent.

"That's exactly what happened," confirmed Wilson. "Everything that Torres said."

"What happened to the gun?" asked Santos, looking at both Torres and Wilson.

"I recall handing it to Miguel, telling him to get rid of it," answered Torres.

Miguel added, "Yes, that's true. I put it in a toolbox in the garage for the moment, but the plan was to take it with me later and dump it. Unfortunately, the auto accident changed everything, and I kind of forgot about the weapon."

"I learned that the FBI got a search warrant," said Scott. "They found the gun and some bloodied rope, and the gun was identified as the murder weapon. They tested the blood and it was Dawson's. They don't have much else to go on right now, but I'll keep my eyes and ears open."

"Yes, keep your lines of communication open to us," said Santos. "I thank you for your discovery. You have saved us a lot of trouble, but I think we will keep a low profile on our West Coast operations for a while. What that means, gentlemen, is that we will need to double up on the East Coast. We are shutting down here for now."

The meeting was adjourned with instructions to report to the safehouse in Miami.

The following day, Wallace arrived in Mexico City for his meeting with Santos. More than anything he needed reassurance that everything was going to continue as before, and the men did their best to assure him it was all handled.

Santos finally asked him, "What are you going to do with the Mountain Gate property? We think you should sell it ASAP."

"I agree," said Wallace. "I'm expecting to be interviewed by the FBI any time now."

Santos advised Wallace to get a lawyer who could act as a buffer.

Santos said, "Let's keep our communications to a minimum for now. We have a man inside the DEA, so I can keep on top of any police progress."

"I'm still scared," stated Wallace.

"Don't be," reassured Torres. "We have your back. I say let's call it a day. I'll drive you back to your hotel."

Chapter 16

After everyone thanked Chief La Greca for dinner, they went on their separate ways with the exception of Celli and Rodriguez. Celli had been waiting for this time alone with Francisco to discuss the issue of jurisdiction in the case. All the evidence pointed towards Dawson's homicide having taken place in L.A., making L.A. the obvious choice for prosecution. However, in this case, the victim was a federal employee which made it a federal crime.

After weighing both sides of the argument, Rodriguez finally said, "Bill, it's all yours."

"Thank you for that, Francisco," replied Celli. "You won't regret that decision. In fact, you have given us the additional motivation we needed to get this case solved."

"Okay, good," said Rodriguez. "I have no doubt. Just keep me informed as things progress."

The following morning, Rodriguez dropped into Homicide to say goodbye as Celli was beginning a meeting with his team of homicide detectives, including Salute and Forman. Fred Wong was also invited because his lab would be key in reviewing the fingerprint records found at the Mountain Gate property, particularly those of Wilson Scott now that he had been identified as a DEA agent.

"I will personally send all the internal information we have on Scott as soon as I arrive back in D.C.," promised Francisco, looking at Wong.

Celli continued the meeting by giving out specific assignments to his detectives. Sandra Salute was charged with interviewing Wallace as soon as he returned from Mexico. Celli's thinking was that he would be his most vulnerable at that time, needing to justify his sudden trip to Mexico. When Celli had called his office to set up the interview, his staff would only say that he was in Mexico and they would let him know when he returned.

Wong's lab had discovered partial prints of Wilson Scott on the murder weapon, along with other prints matching him in and around the house. True to his word, the next day Celli received the files on Scott's background from Rodriguez. The detective hoped the information would shed some light on why he was in the house when Dawson was killed. So far, it was still a mystery.

Celli dove into the pages, hoping for a clue, but the guy appeared clean and on the up and up. Scott had been a close friend of Dawson at West Point, where they met. For some unknown reason, Scott had left West Point in his senior year to join the DEA, at which time he also convinced Dawson to do the same thing. The two men worked and played together until the day Dawson was contacted by the DEA brass and went undercover. The records indicate that

Scott was never told about Dawson's undercover assignment. He worked the drug trade on the East Coast, and, as far as anyone knew, the two of them lost touch with each other. So, back to the big question. What was he doing at the Mountain Gate house?

Celli decided to brainstorm with Forman and Salute on how to approach Wallace.

"He has no history of going dark," said Celli. "I think we need to have a chat with him asap."

"What about Scott?" responded Forman. "He seems to be a prime suspect."

"I'll ask Francisco how we should approach him," said Celli.

When Bill called Francisco, his answer was simple. "I'll advise him that you are investigating the death of his friend Phil Dawson and that you want to get a background on him. Also, since they were close friends, he might have some insight into his death."

"Has Scott been told about Dawson's death?" asked Celli.

"No. There have been no disclosures about his activities or his death," replied Francisco.

"Are you sure?" asked Celli.

"Yes, I'm sure, Bill. In fact, I'm scheduling a meeting with him as head of the Justice Department. We have routine meetings with our personnel, usually when there is a change or a promotion."

"Great. The sooner the better," said Celli.

Casey, Celli's secretary, finally received a call from Wallace's office, indicating that Wallace was back in town and that he would be available the following afternoon at his office if Celli still wanted to meet with him.

Upon hearing the news, Celli said, "Good! Call back and confirm that I'll be there."

Celli arrived, along with Detective Salute, at Wallace's office the next day. Not surprisingly, the penthouse space was plush and boasted a panoramic view of the Pacific Ocean on one side and the mountains on the other. When Celli and Salute walked in, Wallace was seated behind his desk, and standing alongside him was attorney Robert Shapiro of OJ fame.

"I'm not sure why you're here, detectives, but I thought you would have no objection to my attorney being present," said Wallace.

Before Celli could respond, Shapiro jumped in and said, "Bill and I are old friends. I'm sure he doesn't mind."

"That's true," said Celli. "Bob and I are acquainted, and, in fact, I'm glad he is here. You are not a suspect. We just want to get some background into your business with Felix Santos and Felipe

Serena, as well as your connection to the Mountain Gate estate. As you may have heard, we are investigating the death of an individual found in the rear of one of your vehicles which was driven by Filipe Serena. I can ask questions or you can just tell me what you know."

Wallace responded, "I have nothing to hide. About 15 years ago, my company solicited potential investors to invest in some of our real estate projects here in sunny Southern California, which is a hot market. I met Felix and others in Mexico City at one of our presentations, and they became investors and friends over the years. We acquired a residential estate about five years ago to house our out-of-town employees when visiting L.A. and, on occasion, our investors as well when they are visiting here. When the property is occupied, we provide a chef, housekeeping and groundskeepers."

"Can you tell us about Felipe Serena?"

"Yes, his family owns several industrial companies in Mexico. I met them when I met Felix. They have invested heavily in my company. They even asked if I would employ their son who wanted to live in L.A. They hoped that he would eventually attend USC, since I have connections there. He came to work for us a couple of years ago, but he really doesn't do much. I guess we mainly keep him out of his parents' hair. I don't know much about him, and I don't think I've seen him more than a few times. He seems to be a nice kid, likes to chase the ladies. For questions about the residence, you will need to speak with Frank Rauch in my office. He is in charge of the property and responsible for booking the house. To be honest, based upon recent developments, we have decided to sell the property. Can you tell me why the FBI sealed off the place as a crime scene? It's been very embarrassing for me."

"You'll need to speak to them," answered Celli.

"Come on, Bill," said Shapiro. "You need to come straight with us."

"Okay, we believe the person who was discovered in your client's vehicle was killed at the Mountain Gate residence," said Celli. "We also believe that a Mexican drug cartel was responsible for his death."

"What's that got to do with my client," replied the attorney. "You know he's not responsible."

"Maybe not directly, but we know your client is a smart cookie. We think he knows a lot more than he is willing to admit. Let me ask him what was he doing in Mexico over the last few days. I doubt he was on vacation."

"Bill, please give me some time alone with my client," said Shapiro. "You can stay here and we will retreat to his conference room."

As soon as they had left the room, Sandy Salute said, "I think you're making them nervous, Bill."

Twenty minutes later, the lawyer and his client returned. "Okay, my client is totally innocent," stated Shapiro. "Just because some of his investors are from Mexico and Central America that doesn't mean he knows all their backgrounds. Don't put him in the same category as them."

Celli remarked, "Maybe so, but if word got out that drug cartels were investing in his company business, how would that look?"

"Hey, it's not fair to squeeze him," said Shapiro.

"Bob, we are all adults here. Your client wants to save his ass and his business and I understand that," countered Celli. "Can he help us or not?"

"This is all very new to me," said Shapiro. "Can you give us a few days?"

"Yes, of course. Call me when your client is ready to come clean."

Wallace interjected, "I am clean!"

"Well, Mr. Wallace, if you lay down with dogs, you wake up with fleas."

As soon as the detectives had exited Wallace's office, Salute said, "Boss, you were great. You definitely scared the shit out of them."

"Let's wait and see," replied Celli, "but I do think we are getting somewhere."

Chapter 17

Francisco's appointment with Scott was the very next day. Wilson Scott's boss at the DEA had advised him that Francisco Rodriguez from the Justice Department needed to have a conversation with him.

"Do you know what it's about?" asked Scott.

"No idea. Just show up. Maybe it's a promotion!"

Scott arrived on time and was escorted into a conference room on the sixth floor where Francisco was waiting

for him.

After pleasantries, Francisco said, "I

have some sad news for you, Mr. Scott,

and I wanted to personally tell you. Your

friend and college roommate, Phil

Dawson, was murdered in California

about two weeks ago. His body was

discovered in a vehicle involved in an auto

accident. He had been shot in the head.

I'm sorry for your loss. I understand you

were close until he was assigned to an

undercover unit to infiltrate Mexican drug

cartels operating on the West Coast."

Scott sat in silence for a few moments, cradling his face in his hands. Finally, he responded, "How could this happen? I haven't seen or spoken to him in the last five years, but he was a top agent."

"I'm sure it's a shock. I can't give you any details, but I thought you should know."

"Was there a funeral?" asked Scott.

"Not yet," replied Francisco. "We have kept his ID under wraps until our investigation is completed. His family knows and they are devastated, of course. Maybe you should give them a call."

As the two conversed, Francisco looked directly into Scott's eyes. Although the words were right, he didn't detect any real emotion. When Scott left the meeting, he wasn't alone. Francisco had arranged to have him tailed.

Francisco immediately called Celli to report on his interview with Scott. "I was careful not to say anything to Scott that indicated he was a prime suspect in the murder of his friend," he said. "Scott is a good actor. His actions were quite sincere, like a person learning the information for the first time. He is a real cool customer. I have a gut feeling about this guy so I have put him under surveillance. No one knows about this except you. I will keep you fully informed of what we discover. My intuition tells me his involvement goes a great deal further than the murder of Dawson. With your help, maybe we can bring down the house of cards on them all."

"Francisco, I'd be satisfied with just bringing murder charges against him. Anything more is thanks to you, my friend."

Chapter 18

After his conversation with Rodriguez had ended, Celli closed his office door to do some serious thinking. He had to find a way to connect Wallace, Torres and the others in a criminal conspiracy and, at the same time, solve his cold case. If he arrested Scott on the sole murder charge of Dawson, everything else would go away. After sitting in silence, he came up with an idea that just might work.

The detective called Forman and Salute into his office to help him strategize.

"The key might be Scott who was on the cartel's payroll," said Celli. "He must have remorse for killing one of his best friends. he has everything to lose if he doesn't cooperate. Good chance he will be going to prison for the rest of his life and most likely get killed in there. Surely, that's enough incentive to cooperate."

"How do we get the feds to take a step back?" asked Forman.

"I think the government would be very embarrassed that one of their respected DEA agents sold them out to the drug cartel," responded Celli.

Salute said, "I agree, but I think you should first have a confidential conversation with your friend Francisco. If he is on board, then it's a go."

Feeling energized, Celli called Francisco Rodriguez back and filled him in on the plan.

After listening, Francisco said, "Bill, you have my consent, but how are you going to proceed? As you know, the world has ears, and news travels fast, especially if he shows up in your offices."

"I know. I will need to meet with him on the QT."

"I can recall him back to my office, if that's easier for you. That would not raise suspicion. You can meet him here, just the two of you. It's your ballgame," offered Francisco.

"I can't thank you enough," said Celli.

"I hope it works, Bill. I'll keep my fingers crossed."

Francisco Rodriguez was true to his word. Three weeks later he called Celli, simply declaring, "He will be here this Friday. Make your plans!"

Chapter 19

Wilson Scott was already seated in Rodriguez's conference room when Celli walked in.

After introducing the men to each other, Rodriguez said, "I'm going to leave the two of you alone."

After Rodriguez walked out, Scott was visibly confused, but Celli would clear up any confusion momentarily.

Celli, who was recording the conversation, explained in detail his case against Scott while the agent listened in silence.

"I could arrest you and charge you with first-degree murder which carries the death penalty in California," explained Celli. "I'm sure you understand the consequences of your act. It must have hurt you deeply to kill your friend, let alone letting down the DEA and his family. I have a way out for you. I want Santos, Torres, Wallace and the other members of the cartel shut down forever, and you can help me do that. If you do, you will walk. I need you to know I've never done this before, and it's against my nature to let a murderer go. But I have to look at the bigger picture. Are you in or are you out? I need to know right now."

"You are right. I do feel bad about what happened. You have to understand it was either me or him," replied Scott. "I sold out to the cartel a few years back. I can't explain why I did it, but once I was in, there was no way out. I'll do whatever you want. I know it won't bring back Phil, but I owe it to him and his family to try and make it right."

"Okay. This meeting never took place. Go about your business. We will work through Rodriguez, and the next time we meet, be prepared to give me everything you know about the cartel's operations and who was involved. This meeting is now over. Leave by the side door."

Chapter 20

Scott was still shaking when he left the building, but, at the same time, he felt a sense of relief. His secret life was now open to a few who could make a difference.

Just three days later, Scott was back in the fold of the cartel, providing Torres with Coast Guard positions so that their ships could easily slip through without potentially being stopped. This valuable knowledge saved them millions of dollars, and he was paid handsomely for the information.

As Celli had requested, Scott began writing down the events and people in his life since that fateful day he was recruited by the cartel. It would be nearly five years of names, meetings, locations and operations by the cartel that included how the drugs were packaged, the various means of delivery and the contact information of the ultimate drug dealers throughout the United States. His list also included contact numbers and others not necessarily in the cartel but benefited from assisting them. The list included William Wallace who eagerly took their money and invested it in his properties.

Scott had personally witnessed many exchanges between Santos and Wallace over the years.

After Celli returned from Washington, he sat down with his lead detectives, Forman and Salute, to specifically talk about William Wallace.

"I need you two to find out everything you can about William Wallace's business dealings."

Celli's goal was to be fully prepared for the next meeting with Scott. With Forman and Salute concentrating on Wallace, Celli again reviewed the files on the murders of David Gray and Coach Valentine.

After receiving the detectives' report on Wallace, Celli was ready to meet again with Wilson Scott. The following week, Celli, along with his court reporter, was seated across from Scott who was placed under oath. The session took two complete days, and the details Scott revealed were movie worthy. To Celli's surprise, many new characters came into play in Scott's saga.

"Mr. Scott, what do you know about the murders of David Gray and Coach Valentine?" asked the detective, hoping that he would finally be able to tie in the deaths from his cold case.

"Who are they?" asked Wilson Scott. "Sorry, those names are new to me."

"Well then, let me fill you in on the details. It might bring back your memory," responded Celli. "Approximately five years ago, David Gray, the owner of a women's soccer team, the LA Angels, was discovered dead floating in his swimming pool. The autopsy confirmed that it was a homicide. I tried to connect the crime to Robert Torres, the stepfather of Michael Clemens who is a local attorney who represented the team in a dispute. Let's just say that the words passed between Gray and Clemens at the time were of a threatening nature. Not long before Gray was found deceased, we have good reason to believe Gray had threatened Clemens for taking sides with the players because of his sister, Joy Fields, who represented the players union against the owners. However, we could not prove anything. What we do know is that a day or so before his death, Clemens had placed a call to Torres. We believe Torres then ordered the hit. The problem was your department was monitoring Torres' phone calls as part of their investigation into drug smuggling, but they were doing so without a warrant. Unfortunately, we could not use any of the conversations or follow any other evidence that we learned from those conversations. You may be familiar with the fruits of the poisonous tree doctrine. In any event, we are at a dead end."

"What about this Valentine?" asked Scott.

"Valentine was the coach of Gray's soccer team. He had a nasty reputation of sexually assaulting the women players, so when the players union was formed,

Clemens' sister Joy Fields filed complaints about his actions. By this time, Laurie Gray, the wife of David Gray, had acquired ownership of the team and immediately fired Valentine. And, with the help of Clemens, she had him removed from the team's headquarters. On the opening day of soccer season, Valentine showed up drunk and crashed the owner's box waving a gun and threatening to shoot the box occupants which included Laurie Gray, Clemens, his wife and children, as well as Joy Fields. Fortunately, Michael Clemens was able to disarm him and he was arrested, but not without yelling threats towards the occupants as he was being led away. That evening, Clemens called his stepfather Torres and explained Valentine's upsetting and aggressive behavior that day. Again, we could not use the content of their conversation because of your agency's phone taps. However, a day or so later when Valentine was released from custody, he was gunned down just outside of police headquarters by an unknown assailant. It's our belief that Torres ordered that killing as well. I need you to find out, without exposing yourself, if Torres was responsible."

"I remember something about a U.S. women's soccer team being kidnapped in Mexico City from a conversation at Santos' headquarters with some other cartel members. They were talking about how they had rescued them, but I didn't think anything about it. I'll do what I can."

"I appreciate anything you can do, Mr. Scott. We're done for now. Please leave by the side door."

After Scott left the building, Celli excused the court reporter, asking her for the transcript of the meeting before he left for L.A.

"Of course, Detective Celli, you can pick it up from Rodriguez's secretary shortly."

"Great, thank you. Please remember to keep these meetings top secret."

Celli was staying at the Willard Hotel, where he and Rodriguez had planned to meet for dinner that evening. During their dinner conversation, Celli shared a list of names that Scott had given him, which included Wallace and other potential money launderers for the cartel.

"Do you think you could use your influence to persuade the IRS to investigate them for income tax fraud, Francisco?" asked Celli, hoping to attack the cartel from all angles.

Rodriguez winked and smiled as he pocketed the list and replied, "I can't promise anything, Bill."

Celli's flight home was smooth and swift, not unlike his last two days meeting with Scott. He was finally getting somewhere.

Chapter 21

Not long after his meeting with Celli, Scott received a call from Felix Santos. He was to attend an upcoming meeting which would include Santos' lieutenants which meant Torres would be there. The purpose of the meeting was to discuss the reopening of routes on the West Coast, and Santos needed Scott's take on how safe it would be to reopen. For Scott, this would be a perfect time to get information for Celli that would, in turn, save his own ass.

Even though Scott was technically assigned to South Florida, he was taking no chances. He contacted Rodriguez, asking him if he could be reassigned to the L.A. office.

"Please keep your contact with me at a minimum," said Rodriguez, hanging up the phone abruptly. However, a week later his boss called and told him to pack his bags. He had been reassigned to L.A.

Scott smiled to himself thinking that Rodriguez was for real.

Chapter 22

As soon as he arrived in L.A., Scott called Torres.

"Tell Felix I've been transferred to the West Coast and I'm ready to get to work as soon as operations here resume," advised Scott.

Within a week, Torres got back to him. "We will be coming to L.A. to scout routes with you, Wilson," said Torres.

"I think we should meet in San Diego," responded Scott.

"That works. We have a safehouse on Coronado Island."

After Scott's arrival in Los Angeles, the head of the L.A. office contacted him with his first official assignment. He would be partnered with agent Lucas Baker who would show him the ropes. Baker began by taking him through the territory, from Ventura to San Diego. Their job was to work with Border Patrol to follow up on their leads.

During one of their trips to the various border patrol stations, Scott asked Baker where Coronado Island was?

"In San Diego, across the bridge," said Baker.

"Do you know a good place to stay?" asked Scott. "I'm thinking of spending the weekend. I've heard it's a great spot."

"Sure. You'll want to stay at the Del Coronado," answered Baker. "It's a grand old hotel."

"Do you think I could take off on Thursday?"

"Sure. I'll cover for you. If anything of importance arrives, I'll give you a call."

Scott knew he needed to be very careful to cover his tracks. Late Thursday afternoon, he rented a car and drove down to San Diego to the address that

Torres had given him for the safehouse. When he arrived, he was surprised that Torres had brought along four of his underlings—Joey Medina, Art Ramos, David Molina and Alfred Lopez.

When the discussions began, Scott explained that the land routes were a lot safer than the water routes, and that he had been meeting with the border patrol agents at their various stations along the California/Mexico border.

"In a week or so, I should be able to give you the safest routes," said Scott.

Torres was pleased to share the information with Santos. "Get your distributors ready to receive product!"

Over the next couple of days, they partied, with Torres and his crew showing Scott around and taking him to their favorite Mexican restaurants in the area. The tequila flowed, and eventually the conversation turned to soccer. Art Ramos was laughing over how they had taken down the owner and a coach of a women's soccer team years back.

Torres turned to Scott and said, "If you ever need Lopez or Ramos, their services are there for you, friend."

"I'm not a soccer fan," replied Scott.

"Well, we are big fans," responded Torres. "In fact, we once saved the U.S. Women's Soccer Team from being kidnapped."

"That sounds dangerous," stated Scott.

"Not really. You see, my daughter was with the team at the time and I was concerned for her safety."

By Sunday, when the meetings and partying came to an end, Wilson Scott knew he was on to something big for Celli.

Chapter 23

Two weeks passed before Scott's next contact with Torres.

"Roberto, your people should use the border crossing at El Centro," began the agent. "It's a farming community and you can come up through the desert by the Salton Sea. The border patrol manning that station are old-school, not young eager beavers trying to make a name for themselves."

He then followed up with a call to Rodriguez, asking him to set up a meeting with Celli.

The next day, Scott valet parked at the Beverly Hills Hotel. As he walked in, Celli was waiting for him in the lobby. There was only eye contact between the two as Scott followed Celli to a bank of elevators. Stepping in, they rode up to the sixth floor and entered room 614. Already waiting there for them was a court reporter to record the meeting.

Scott shared the information he gleaned from the weekend in Coronado. Celli could not believe what he was hearing. The information far exceeded his expectations. No doubt, if what the agent was saying was true, it was a major coup.

This not only confirmed his belief that Torres was responsible for the deaths of Gray and Valentine, he now knew the names of the actual killers. He also now knew the routes and methods the cartel was going to use to enter the United States. Scott reported that they were planning to use gasoline tankers to transport the drugs.

When the meeting concluded, Scott rode the elevator down alone and returned to his vehicle.

Celli couldn't wait to contact Rodriguez with the news. He gave him the drug routes for the feds to use or not.

"Francisco, it's their business, not mine. I've got the information to solve my murders, although I do hope the DEA stops the cartel," said Celli. "By the way, do you know how the IRS investigation is going? I would love to see Wallace in handcuffs. It might discourage others from cleaning drug money."

"To be honest, I'm trying to stay clear of their work. I'll check back with you later about anything I find out."

Chapter 24

Celli had Steinberg, his department's computer whiz, run the names Scott had given him through every social network. That drew a blank, as did the FBI database. However, Homeland Security was another story. It offered records of work visas issued to each one of them, allowing them to enter the U.S. The records also revealed their entries into the U.S. were just prior to Gray's killing and when Valentine was hit.

Celli now had enough evidence to present to Chief La Greca, hoping to get his okay to go to the DA. La Greca agreed.

After the DA reviewed Celli's murder book, he said, "You're going to need to protect your source as much as possible, detective. The only way to do that is by a grand jury indictment. You can use your informant's statements under oath. You have Homeland Security records showing they were in the U.S. at the time of the murders, plus your investigative reports on the murders themselves, including the crime lab reports. I think I can secure no-bail arrest warrants and the indictments issued under seal.

Twenty days later, the Grand Jury met and authorized the filing of an indictment charging murder in the first degree.

Celli was now armed with warrants which included Roberto Torres. All he needed now was the cooperation of Homeland Security to advise him when the men crossed over the border again into the U.S.

The prior history showed they used various entry points, and Celli knew that without that information he would have no way of knowing their whereabouts to execute the warrants. All border agents were alerted but told not to make any arrests of the individuals, only to immediately notify Celli by using a special

number to call.

Chapter 25

Just three days later, all hell broke loose at the San Ysidro border crossing. A vehicle which was following a gasoline tanker truck was stopped. The two individuals in the car were later identified as Joey Medina and Art Ramos. Instead of passing them through the crossing, they were ordered to step out of the car. That's when the driver opened fire on the border agent, killing him and injuring another agent who returned fire and killed the driver.

The passenger was arrested without injury. The driver was Art Ramos.

When Rodriguez called Celli, notifying him about the incident, the detective was outraged.

"Who the fuck trains your people?" yelled Celli into the phone. "And where is the other occupant of the car? I want him turned over to me now!"

"Bill, you will get your man. I can assure you this will never happen again," said Francisco.

The news had also gotten back to Santos. Thankfully, the tanker filled with drugs had made it through the crossing. He directed Torres to check into the story.

And find out what really happened.

"Was Ramos driving, and who fired his weapon at the border agent? I want to know where Medina is right now, ask Wilson to find out the truth and the whereabouts of Medina."

After Torres contacted him, Scott called Rodriguez who told him what had played out at the border.

"Ramos died in the firefight, Medina was taken into custody and is now in Celli's hands," said Rodriguez.

Scott repeated the story to Torres leaving out the whereabouts of Medina.

He merely indicated that he was still "in

the system".

Chapter 26

Celli was still angry when Medina was delivered to his custody. He'd already met with Chief La Greca and DA Ellis who explained the next steps.

"Medina has a right to legal counsel, plus he needs to be arraigned on the murder charge within 48 hours," said Ellis.

"That could ruin our ability to catch the other defendants in the indictment," added La Greca.

"We can avoid that by having the U.S. Attorney charge him with illegal entry into the country," suggested Ellis.

"Why didn't I think of that?" said Celli.

"I'll talk with the U.S. Attorney in charge and explain our dilemma," offered Ellis.

Medina was later transferred to the Federal Detention Center to wait for the filing of federal charges. The word reached Torres of Medina's whereabouts which he immediately shared with Santos. Santos was relieved. Maybe the incident at the border was an isolated one, but he wanted to make sure that Medina would keep his mouth shut.

Attorney Ted Anderson was appointed by the court to represent Medina, but the inmate refused to speak with him. Anderson was informed that there was also a hold on his client by the state based upon a sealed indictment obtained through the L.A. DA's office. He attempted to find out what the charges were without success, and was even more confused when he received a phone call from Roberto Torres asking him to stall the case as long as possible.

In the meantime, Celli had attempted to access Medina without luck. Since he had legal representation, Celli would have to go through his clueless

attorney.

Chapter 27

After the incident at the border, the cartel made the decision to shut down all West Coast deliveries for the time being. Everything would be going through the East Coast until things cooled down. When Celli found out about the cartel's decision, he was pissed knowing that he had lost his prey. Then again, he thought, if they were not coming to him, he could go to them. But how was he going to track these guys down in Mexico? He would definitely need Wilson Scott's assistance to make this new plan work.

Celli knew it was not the time to get Francisco involved, but luckily, he did have Wilson Scott's private phone number for an emergency. This fit the category. That evening as he drove home, he called the number.

Scott answered and was surprised to hear Celli's voice on the other end of the line.

"I have a special request, Wilson. I need to meet with you as soon as possible."

"That will be difficult. I have work assignments during the week."

"I understand," said Celli. "How about Saturday afternoon? I can meet you on the Redondo Beach Pier in the front of Tony's. Bring some fishing gear, and we can talk at the end of the pier while fishing. But listen, no one is to know about this meeting, especially not Francisco."

"What's this about?" asked Scott.

"You'll find out on Saturday."

Saturday arrived, and Celli packed up his fishing gear and drove to the pier. On Saturdays, it was usually packed with weekend fishermen, with luck the detective found a space on the pier and set up his fishing gear putting his bait bucket in front of a bench. He asked the fisherman next to his spot if he would keep an eye on his gear for a few moments. As soon as he reached the front of Tony's, he spotted Wilson Scott. When he had gotten his attention, Celli signaled him to follow him back to his fishing spot. Scott quickly set up next to him, and the two men cast their lines into the water, took a seat on the bench and waited for a bite.

When he was confident no one was within hearing range, Celli explained his plan. "I want to kidnap Torres, Ayala and Medina from Mexico and smuggle them back across the border so that I can arrest them."

Scott's reaction was one of horror. "Are you crazy? It's not possible. Who is going to do that for you? I don't know a soul who would do it for any amount of money."

"What about a rival cartel gang? Aren't they always fighting with each other for territory?"

"Yes, but Santos is Mexican Mafia. They are the big cheese."

"Well, think harder. He must have enemies."

"Not a chance this will work," stated Scott. "You are out of your league, detective."

"I have gone the extra mile for you," responded Celli.

"And, if there was any way to pull this off, I'd be your man."

Celli glanced at Scott's line running out. "Hey, you've caught something!"

Scott reeled in a small perch, but he was not smiling as he packed up his gear and left the detective on the pier.

Celli just sat there soaking up the Saturday afternoon sun and digesting what the agent had told him. He was glad he had not shared his plan with anyone else. There had to be another way.

Chapter 28

When Celli arrived at his office on Monday morning, there was a note on his desk to call the DA Ellis. Celli couldn't wait to hear what he had to say.

"Bill, I have some bad news," said Ellis.

"Why? What's going on?" asked Celli.

"I received a call from U.S. Attorney Barron. He told me that Medina's attorney has filed a motion to dismiss the case, which on further review seems to have merit. His argument states that since

Medina had a visa to enter the United States, he can't be charged with illegal entry. He spoke to his boss and he was of the same opinion, therefore, their office is going to dismiss the case. That means he will be released from custody within a day or so. Since we have a hold on him, they will turn him over to us. So, Bill, what do you want to do? Without time waivers, everyone is going to know what charges we filed and what evidence we have if we go forward. Scott would have to testify, which would disclose his role in all of this and further give the other defendants a heads up. I suggest we recall the hold and let him walk, but it's your case and it's your decision."

"Shit! If we recall the hold and just let him walk, what does that do to our case against him and the others?" asked Celli.

"Nothing," said Ellis. "It's still alive. All you need to do is catch all of the suspects, then we can proceed."

Celli was stunned by the development. I'm batting zero, he thought. Scott had pooh-poohed his plan and now this.

"I guess you should go ahead and tell Barron to dismiss the case," responded the detective.

After he hung up the phone, he sat at his desk feeling thoroughly beaten down. Detective Salute looked in and saw her boss with an unusual look of defeat.

"Are you okay?" she asked.

He invited her in and explained the recent developments that had him down.

"Bill, don't get depressed over this," said Salute. "We win a lot of the time, but we can't win them all."

"But, Sandy, I have the evidence to convict those bastards. I appreciate the pep talk, but this is so frustrating."

"Why don't you put a tail on Medina when he gets released?"

"It's a good idea, but I can't do that if he crosses the border into Mexico, which is sure to happen."

"Do you remember Gabe Abbott and Shawn Bennett who retired from SWAT a few years back? They are now working for Blackwell Contractors. I think you know Jerry Shuman who heads up their Western division."

"Sure, but what can they do for us?"

"Lots! They can go anywhere they want. If you assign them to tail, borders would not be a problem. And better yet, they are fluent in Spanish. Why don't you have a chat with the Chief? It might be in the budget."

Celli responded, "I've run out of ideas. I have nothing to lose. Thanks, Sandy."

Celli laid out the situation to Chief La Greca, his conversation with DA Ellis and Salute's idea of using Abbott and Bennett who now work for Blackwell.

"We know them, Chief. They were in SWAT with Jerry Shuman who now heads up the company. Question is, do we have the funds to cover such an operation?"

La Greca replied, "Yes, we might depending on how much we're talking about?"

"Could you give Shuman a call and discuss what we need?" asked Celli. "We need to act fast. Medina will be released within a day or two."

"I understand. Stay here for a minute," responded the Chief as he punched in Shuman's number on the phone. About ten minutes into the call, the Chief turned to Celli and gave him a thumbs up.

Hanging up, the Chief said, "You're covered. Blackwell's West Coast offices are in Long Beach; here's the address. Get over there now. They're waiting for you."

Celli smiled and said, "Chief, I could kiss you."

"That won't be necessary. Now, get the hell out of here!"

Chapter 29

Attorney Ted Anderson was seated in the conference room of the Federal Detention Facility, waiting for the arrival of his client. Joey Medina was brought in by two U.S. Marshals and took a seat across from Anderson, without saying a word.

"It's okay. You don't have to speak," said Anderson. "However, you might like to know that U.S. Attorney is going to dismiss your case. In fact, I expect you will be released from here within two days once the judge signs off on the dismissal.

Is there someone you want me to call about your release?"

A big smile came across Medina's face at hearing his attorney's words. "Thank you for all of your efforts," said Medina. "When you find out the date of my release, I can call someone to pick me up."

Anderson agreed to keep him informed. While the attorney was meeting with Medina, Celli and Salute were at Blackwell's West Coast headquarters meeting with Shuman, whom they both knew from the early days when he was with the LAPD. Celli had brought all the files with him that explained in detail the targets of their tail and specifically what he wanted Bennett and Abbott to do. They were to follow Medina upon his release to whatever destination he chose.

"I believe it will be Mexico," explained Celli. "Once there, I need you to locate the others and kidnap them. Just bring them back to U.S. soil so I can make the arrests."

At this point in the meeting, Bennett and Abbott entered the room. Neither Salute nor Celli had seen the two for years. It was a warm welcome. The men were now in their middle 50s, collecting retirement from LAPD and now earning big bucks as mercenary contractors. Once they were filled in on Celli's instructions, they were on board.

"Medina is being released from the federal facility within the next day or so," stated Celli. "You should be able to pick up the tail then. It would be best if you only communicated with Shuman. I'll get all my information from him. Good luck and good hunting!"

Chapter 30

When Shawn Bennett contacted an old friend in the U.S. Marshal's office to find out when Medina was scheduled to be released, he was alarmed with the news. Medina was already being processed and would likely be released within a couple of hours. That would not give him much time to get there, and the possibility of missing Medina's release would jeopardize the entire plan.

Running out of the building, Bennett jumped into his car and hauled ass down the 110 Freeway to downtown

L.A. During the drive, he called Abbott and told him what was going on and that he hoped to be at the jail before Medina got out the door.

"I'll call you back once I make contact," he promised.

Thirty minutes later, Joey Medina was standing on the sidewalk in front of the Federal Building waiting for his ride just as Bennett drove up and parked his car in a red zone about 20 feet from where Medina was standing. Bennett put his former police badge on the dashboard, feeling thankful that it still worked for parking in no parking areas.

He watched as a car pulled up in just minutes and Medina slid into the backseat.

Bennett immediately identified the vehicle as an UBER ride. It left the curb and drove off in the direction of the Santa Monica Freeway, with Bennett following behind. Entering the westbound lanes, the UBER soon exited at Lincoln Boulevard in Santa Monica and deposited Medina in front of a high-rise condo building at the corner of Pico and Ocean Blvd.

Bennett used his phone to take photos as Medina entered the lobby.

Pulling into a circular driveway fronting the building, Bennett flashed his badge at the valet who pointed to a nearby area to park. Next, he called Abbott and gave him the location.

"I'll head out right now. It shouldn't take me more than 45 minutes to get there," responded his partner.

Bennett decided to enter the lobby of the ritzy condo building. A young woman was seated behind a counter and a security guard lingered on the other side of the lobby. He decided to see what he could find out about Medina's destination.

Smiling, Bennett leaned over the counter and said, "I'm hoping you can help me out. An individual just came in here and I was delayed parking the car. I am part of his security detail and he was supposed to wait in the lobby for me. I really need to locate him." Bennett pulled out his credentials for her to inspect.

"Yes, he just went up," said the woman.

"Can you please tell me where? I could be in a lot of trouble if I don't find him right away. I am responsible for his safety."

"I understand," she replied, looking serious. "He went to unit 1210 on the 12th floor."

"Thank you," said Bennett. "You're a life saver. I promise I didn't hear that from you. By the way, do you know whose condo it is?"

"Sure. It belongs to the William Wallace Investment Company. You probably know they also own this building."

"Yes, of course," he replied. "Say, would you mind if I waited in the lobby for my partner? He should be here soon."

"Okay, but please make yourself invisible. Other owners might question who you are."

Bennett agreed and disappeared around a corner to report in to Shuman. As agreed, Shuman then called Celli and explained the status of Medina and the tail, including the fact that Medina was at Wallace's condo.

"They will keep him under surveillance and see who visits him or where he goes," said Shuman.

When Medina entered the condo, he found clothes, food, a bar full of alcohol, toiletries and a cell phone waiting for him. Instructions were placed next to the phone that told Medina to stay put until further instructions from Roberto Torres. The note warned that he could have been followed.

Abbott arrived as promised, and the two took turns watching the entrance and exits of the building. At this point, all they could do was wait for some movement by Medina.

Chapter 31

Medina was waiting, too. Finally, the phone rang the next morning. It was Roberto Torres.

"I hope you like the accommodations," said Torres.

"Wow! I never expected this," replied Medina.

"Well, enjoy it while it lasts," said Torres. "I expect to get you out of there and on your way home in the next few days. Listen, Santos wants me to ask you what happened at the border."

"It all happened so fast," replied Medina. "I remember that Art thought they were going to stop the tanker. He yelled something out the window to the border guards. I can't recall exactly what he said, but two border guards came over to our car with their guns drawn. Then, Art pulled his gun out and started firing at them. The tanker crossed the border. Both guards were hit, but before they went down, they returned fire hitting Art. Other guards came up to my side of the car and grabbed me, pulling me out of the car and throwing me to the ground. They handcuffed me. To this day, I've never uttered a word about any of it."

"You're a good soldier," said Torres.

Three more days passed and Medina had not shown. Bennett and Abbott were getting tired and decided to contact Shuman.

"We can't stay here forever," said Bennett. "There's been zero movement by Medina and no one has gone in or out of the condo."

"Let me check in with Celli. I'll get back to you."

Celli and Shuman agreed that the agents should give it another day or two and if there was no movement, the surveillance should be called off. Celli also thought that his own detectives could take over the surveillance.

Celli was getting concerned, but the next day his prayers were answered. A black Cadillac limo pulled up in front of the condo building. Five minutes later, Medina emerged from the elevator and quickly entered the waiting limo. The limo wasted no time departing, with Abbott following at a safe distance. It wasn't long before the limo pulled into the Santa

Monica Airport, turning off of Centinela and driving into the area where the private planes were parked. He observed stairs being lowered from one of the private jets as the limo pulled up to it. Medina quickly bounded out, climbing the stairs and disappearing inside the aircraft.

Abbott was able to jot down the make, model and serial number of the plane before it took off. Just minutes later, it taxied down the runway and jetted away. By this time, Bennett had caught up with Abbott. They called Shuman and reported Medina's swift, choreographed departure.

When Celli got the news, he was frustrated. Nothing seemed to be going his way. He called Steinberg, his tech specialist, to run down the plane's registration information. He was able to get back quickly, and, no surprise, the jet was registered to William Wallace. Celli knew he could not touch Wallace at this point, so he took the next best avenue. He instructed Jerry Forman to deal with air traffic control to obtain a flight plan for the jet.

"Sorry to tell you, boss," said the detective. "The flight plan says the destination is Mexico City."

Celli shook his head. "Fuck, fuck, fuck."

Chapter 32

Wilson Scott's phone rang. It was Torres informing him that Medina had been released from custody and was now in Mexico City. "Santos wants you to find out why the sudden release," said Torres. "He is concerned that maybe Medina is cooperating with authorities."

"I'll make it a priority to find out," promised Scott.

"If the incident at the border was truly an isolated incident, maybe we could resume operations," added Torres. "When you get information on Medina,

Mr. Santos would like you to fly down and report to him face-to-face."

"Just give me a few days to investigate," replied Scott.

After hanging up, Scott called Celli, bypassing Rodriguez, to set up a meeting. Two days later, Scott showed up at the LA Athletic Club on Spring Avenue to collaborate with Celli who had arranged for a private meeting room.

When Scott walked in, he was greeted by an elderly gray-haired man at the front desk. Scott identified himself as

Charles Johnson, the guest name Celli had given him.

"Yes, Mr. Johnson, take the elevator to the second floor. I believe that's where Mr. Celli said he would be meeting you."

Scott exited the elevator which opened up to a spacious lounge and bar area decorated with heavy tables and oversized leather chairs. Celli had been watching the elevator, and when Scott exited, he jumped up from his overstuffed chair, a scotch in one hand and waving with the other.

As Scott approached the detective, Celli asked, "What are you drinking?"

Scott replied, "Belvedere vodka on the rocks with a splash of cranberry juice. Thanks!"

When his drink arrived, they retreated to a private room adjacent to the bar area. Once seated, Celli asked, "Okay, what's the emergency? I hope it's good news. We certainly need some."

Scott repeated what Torres had asked of him. "They need a reply from me, so what's the story going to be?"

Celli explained that the U.S. Attorney had dropped the charges because Medina had a visa allowing him to enter the U.S. "They had an air-tight defense. When he was released, I tried to put a tail on him, but that backfired too. You can tell Mr. Santos and whoever else that needs to know, that the border incident has been closed. I'm now sitting here with my dick in my hand with nothing to show for my efforts to bring those responsible to justice."

"Listen, I can help to reopen the West Coast so maybe you're not dead yet," offered Scott.

"This has turned into one of my toughest cases," confessed Celli. "It's exasperating when you know the perps and you've got warrants for their arrest, but you're still empty handed."

"I'm doing my best. Let's not give up now."

"Okay... how about another drink?"

"Not for me. I'm technically still on duty," replied Scott. "I'll be in touch."

A week later, Wilson Scott was seated opposite Santos and Torres in Santos' hacienda just outside of Mexico

City. Scott explained, in detail, what he'd found out from his sources at the DEA.

"Medina is off the hook, and never said a word. After reviewing the evidence, the charges were dismissed," said Scott. "I imagine Medina has already told you what happened at the border. From my point of view, you can reopen the West Coast at your convenience."

Santos said, "Thank you, Wilson. I'm so relieved to hear you say that. It's been costing me millions of dollars each month while we were shut down. By the way, I want to invite you to attend a boxing match. My son is fighting for the heavyweight championship of the world in Las Vegas at Caesar's Palace next month. He's undefeated and is training hard for this fight. I've arranged for four suites at Caesars, so please come as my guest. I'm so proud of my son Mario Junior that I've invited all the crew to attend."

"It would be my pleasure. Thank you for the invite!" replied Scott.

Chapter 33

When Wilson Scott arrived back in L.A., he was anxious to contact Celli. He knew his invitation to attend Mario Santos heavyweight bout in Las Vegas on May 27th would be good news for the detective. He also knew that Celli would be happy to hear that everyone would be there, at least everyone Celli cared about right now. It looked like Celli's luck was changing.

Chapter 34

Scott was right about Celli's reaction to the news. He could have sworn he was tearing up. Celli called Forman, Salute and four other homicide detectives to his office to share the good news and make a plan.

"This is probably our one and only chance and we can't fuck this up," said Celli to his group of detectives. "The fight takes place just thirty days from now, so we need to stay on top of this."

"I have a good friend who is the assistant chief of police in Las Vegas," volunteered Forman. "We're going to need his help."

"Good," responded Celli. "I went through police training with Ben Wells who is now with the Nevada State Police so I think we are covered in Nevada. First, let's find out what the authorities need from us, and also, we are going to need some seats in the boxing arena as close as possible to where Santos will be sitting."

"I think I can handle that," responded Forman. "My friend Steven is very close to Caesar's Palace security personnel."

"Okay! Let's move on this. No time to waste," instructed Celli.

Three weeks passed quickly. After several meetings with the Vegas authorities, everything seemed to be in order. The closer the fight day approached, the more nervous and preoccupied Celli became. He knew this was his last chance.

Celli with his detectives, along with the Nevada authorities, had suite reservations at the MGM Grand. They had tickets for the fight that were usually reserved for the resort's high rollers. Celli had provided the arrest warrants to the

Las Vegas DA and everything was in order.

The fight was now three days away. The

agreed upon plan was to wait for the fight

to end and then make the

arrests.

Chapter 35

It was now just two days until fight night. Celli, Salute, Forman and three other detectives, along with four officers from the SWAT unit caravanned to Las Vegas, arriving at the MGM Grand Hotel late afternoon. Celli's goal was to keep out of sight as much as possible. He couldn't run the risk of running into anyone who was a part of the Santos entourage. After they checked in, Celli contacted his friend Ben Wells of the Nevada State Police advising him that they were on site.

"I think we should review our plans for the takedown," said Wells.

"I would also like you to meet my second in command," responded Celli. "How do you want to do this?"

"I could meet you and Detective Forman in the lounge bar at 6 p.m.," suggested Wells. "We don't need a crowd and I don't want to attract attention. Also, no alcohol on the job."

At the bar, Wells explained, "I will have six of my state troopers pose as ushers in the arena where Santos and his group will be sitting."

"My team's seating is on both sides of the aisle leading up to the ring in Santos' section," said Celli.

When the fight is over, my people will escort the Santos group out of the arena first, before the crowd exits," explained Wells. "As they walk down the aisle towards the exit, your people will follow and make the arrests. I want to make sure the public stays out of harm's way."

Then Wells produced a map of the arena marking the exact seating locations for Santos' group, as well as Celli's people. Handing the seating chart to Celli, he said,

"Bill, I hope this goes smoothly. I don't want anyone getting hurt."

"Don't worry, Ben. My team is very professional. I don't expect any trouble."

Wells stood, thanking the detectives for the meeting. "I'll see you Friday at the arena. I think we should all be there at 5 p.m. for a walk through. The fights start at 7 p.m., and we should be in our seats by 6:30. I'm sure that Santos and his entourage will be showing up sometime after the preliminary fights and before main event begins, probably around 9 p.m."

Chapter 36

Felix Santos, Roberto Torres and their entourage, which included Wilson Scott, Joey Medina, Miguel Ayala, Alfred Lopez and four others, arrived at McCarran Field on a private jet where three limousines were waiting to transport them to Caesars on the morning of the fight. Celli was relieved to find out they had all checked in, as reported by Ben Wells' officers who had posed as hotel employees stationed in the lobby.

After completing the planned walk-through at 5 p.m., Forman and Celli had a good sense of where the players would be. Six o'clock rolled around quickly. Celli and his group, all dressed in civilian clothing, left the MGM in various taxis, with no more than two per taxi. Twenty minutes later, they were standing at the entrance of the Sports Arena. As expected, Wells' officers were posed as ushers who escorted them to their seats. When they first arrived, the crowd was still very thin, however they knew the fight was a sellout and had merited full coverage on ESPN.

As the arena filled up, Santos' people had still not made an appearance. After the first fight was over, they finally appeared, proceeding down the aisle to their seats. Celli could breathe again; everything was falling into place.

The undercard fights finished as expected around 9 p.m. Right on cue, a man hurried down the aisle wearing a shirt emblazoned with "Santos" on the back. He stopped at the front row where Felix. was sitting and motioned for him to get up and join him. The two men then walked together towards the back of the arena.

Celli was alarmed and exchanged panicked looks with Forman. Seated on the aisle, he waved over an usher who explained that the person who contacted Felix. was Hank Friedman who was his son's manager and trainer. He was taking him to the fighter's dressing room to see his son before the fight. That seemed logical to Celli who calmed down and waited for things to begin.

He did not have to wait long. A half hour later, the crowd started to roar as the fighters strutted down the aisle towards the ring, backed by an extravaganza of loud music and dancing girls. When it was time for Mario to make his grand entrance, his father walked by his side until they reached the ring. Felix retreated to his seat. The introductions lasted for another twenty minutes, which gave Celli time to observe the audience, which included movie stars, sports personalities and many other high-profile public figures.

The bell finally rang, signaling the beginning of the first round. Although Celli had instructed his people to keep their eyes on the cartel group, not the fight, it was difficult to ignore the wild competition happening in front of them, not to mention the screaming fans. Finally, in the 10th round, Mario. caught his opponent with a left hook, knocking him down for the count.

The crowd was on its feet, screaming, applauding and waving Mexican flags. After the crowd was seated, Celli watched two of the ushers approach Felix. The detective knew what they were saying: he would need to leave now, before the crowd, to be able to join his son. Santos agreed, standing. His entourage also stood and followed Santos, walking towards the rear exit of the arena.

As soon as they reached the exit, the group was ambushed by Celli's officers as well as Nevada State Police officers who were waiting. Santos, Torres and three others were singled out.

"What the hell is going on?" yelled Santos.

Torres, Medina, Ayala and Lopez were handcuffed and moved to a room near the concession stand. Scott was standing next to Santos and whispered in his ear, "Let's get out of here. I'll made some calls and get some straight answers."

Celli soon joined the confused arrestees and explained what was happening.

"You are being charged with the murders of David Gray and Coach Valentine."

No one said a word other than wanting to contact their lawyers.

Celli suddenly felt overwhelmed. This had been a long time coming. In fact, at times he thought this moment would never arrive. Justice had worked in his favor and two cases were finally at a close.

Jerry Forman couldn't help but smile. "Bill, Sgt. Preston of the Royal Canadian police always got his man," said Forman, "and so do you! Congratulations!"

ABOUT THE AUTHOR

Carl K. Osborne is a successful criminal defense trial lawyer, in practice for over fifty years. He grew up in a Hollywood family who were involved in the entertainment business in one way or another. His Mother was an Olympian, participating in the 1936 Olympic games in Berlin and later became an actress. And he was on the 1984 Olympic Advisory Committee. His Father was a financier and later a published poet. His Uncle was the late British movie actor James Mason. He started his writing career in the early 90's as a hobby. It now occupies a lot more of his time. He has previously published seventeen books including:

Out of Bounds, Super Notes, Short Stories, Retribution, O'Neil's Law, O'Neil For the Defense, Backfired, A Questionable Hero, Broken Shields, Hollywood Murders, Twisted Justice, Outfoxed, Unwanted Advances, The Wrong Side of Humanity, No Peace Behind The Badge, The Game Changer and The Yellow Card.